MINNOW and ROSE

An Oregon Trail Story

Written by JUDY YOUNG

Illustrated by BILL FARNSWORTH

SLEEPING BEAR PRESS
TALES *of* YOUNG AMERICANS SERIES

For my daughter,
Brett,
Girl-With-Imagination

and in memory of my mother
who had beautiful red hair.

JUDY

❧

For Aimee

BILL

Text Copyright © 2009 Judy Young
Illustration Copyright © 2009 Bill Farnsworth

All rights reserved. No part of this book may be reproduced in any manner
without the express written consent of the publisher, except in the case of brief
excerpts in critical reviews and articles. All inquiries should be addressed to:

Sleeping Bear Press
310 North Main Street, Suite 300
Chelsea, MI 48118
www.sleepingbearpress.com

© 2009 Sleeping Bear Press is an imprint of Gale, a part of Cengage Learning.

Printed and bound in China.

First Edition

10 9 8 7 6 5 4 3 2 1

Library of Congress Cataloging-in-Publication Data

Young, Judy.
Minnow and Rose : an Oregon trail story
/ written by Judy Young ; illustrated by Bill Farnsworth.
p. cm.
Summary: Traveling west with her pioneer family in a wagon
train, Rose meets Minnow, who lives in a Native American village
along the banks of a river.
ISBN 978-1-58536-421-3
[1. Wagon trains—Fiction. 2. Frontier and pioneer life—Fiction.
3. Indians of North America—Fiction. 4. Rescues—Fiction.
5. Friendship—Fiction.] I. Farnsworth, Bill, ill. II. Title.
PZ7.Y8664Mi 2009
[E]—dc22   2008024768

Author's Note

I have often driven across the western plains and there's never been a time I didn't think of the days of the Oregon Trail. It's obvious with the present-day roads, farms, and towns that it doesn't look as it did in the mid-1800s but there is still an awesome ruggedness that stretches across the never-ending prairie. It was on a drive from Missouri to Idaho that I first thought about the story that became *Minnow and Rose*.

In writing *Minnow and Rose*, I not only wanted to show a glimpse of life on the trail, but also the positive relationship that often existed between the pioneers and the Native Americans. During the early days of the Oregon Trail, encounters between the two cultures were often business transactions, bartering goods such as tools, livestock, food, and other merchandise for services. One service frequently documented was help at river crossings.

Today, we easily zoom across rivers on bridges, but to the pioneers river crossings were laborious and dangerous. Wagon trains often took several days to cross just one river. Sometimes wagons toppled over and pioneers not only lost their belongings, but also their lives. In 1857 at least 37 people drowned crossing the Green River in present-day Wyoming. There are also documented accounts of Native Americans saving pioneers from drowning.

I also wanted *Minnow and Rose* to illustrate that children are children no matter what cultures they come from. Children are universally inquisitive about others and curious about their differences, but overall they want to make friends and be accepted.

And so I created the fictional characters, Minnow and Rose, who would meet at a river crossing. The river became a metaphor for both the division between cultures, as well as where those cultures met and flowed together as one.

Her name was Girl-Who-Comes-With-Berries, but everyone called her Minnow.

She was supposed to be born when heat waves in the grasses, but came early during days of juicy berries. Minnow was small even though she had seen ten seasons of berry picking, but she could swim like a fish. She was constantly thinking of ways to get in the water. When sent to pick berries, Minnow often crawled through the prickly branches and slipped unnoticed into the river that ran alongside the village. But today she wanted to float down the rapids.

"Can I go to the crossing spot?" Minnow asked. "There are lots of berries to pick there."

"Yes, but be careful," said her mother.

Minnow grabbed a basket.

Minnow followed the river upstream and got busy picking.
Suddenly, she became aware of noises. They were different
from the river's song.

Peeking through the leaves, she saw covered wagons forming
a circle on the other side of the river. Minnow knew what
that meant. Strangers were coming across the prairie again!

Rose walked beside the wagon, wishing something exciting would happen. For over a month they had traveled across the never-ending prairie. Every day was the same. When the horn blew at five, they got up, ate, packed, and moved on.

Today seemed no different than the others. But in mid-morning the wagon train started to circle up.

"Why are we stopping?" Rose asked.

"There's a river ahead," said Pa. "We'll set up camp and cross tomorrow."

"Good," said Ma. "We need to wash. Look at Rose's hair!"

Rose had been named for her shocking red hair. Now, like everything else, it was covered with dust kicked up by the oxen.

"I'll fetch some water," Rose said, grabbing a bucket.

The river rushed deep and fast. Rose walked downstream. Soon the rapids slowed to a still pool. There, Rose found a wonderful surprise. Big, juicy berries!

Rose crawled through the thorny branches, putting berries in her bucket until she reached the water's edge. She stuck her head into the river and her hair returned to its coppery color. When she raised her head, she heard noises. It sounded like camp, but it was coming from the other side of the river.

Rose peered across. There was a camp. But there were no covered wagons in this camp. Across the river were teepees. Rose knew what that meant. Indians!

"I must tell Father about the wagons!" Minnow thought.

Minnow put her basket into the rushing water and jumped in. As she floated alongside the basket, she saw a girl running along the bank. Minnow had never seen a girl like this one. Her hair was the color of the setting sun. The girl stopped and looked down at Minnow. Their eyes met. The red-haired girl had eyes like the summer sky.

Rose had been running as fast as she could, following the river upstream. She needed to tell Pa about the teepees. Suddenly, something strange caught her eye. She stopped and stared at the water. A basket floated down the river. But that wasn't all. Alongside the basket was a girl with pitch-black hair. The girl in the river had eyes as dark as a moonless night.

Minnow reached her village and ran to her father. "Wagons like the ones that came last year are at the crossing!" she said excitedly.

"We should go meet them," Father said. "Perhaps they need our help to cross the river."

As the men gathered and mounted their horses, Father told Minnow to go home. But Minnow wanted to see the red-haired girl again.

"It would show you come in friendship if a child came with you, Father," she said. Then, as an afterthought, she added, "I am the one who saw them first."

Father looked sternly at Minnow but lifted her onto the back of his horse. "When we get there, stay on the horse," he commanded.

Minnow's father led the way to the crossing spot. The horses plunged into the water and swam across. A group of men stood near the wagons, watching them arrive.

Women and children peeked out from behind the wagons' dusty covers. As Father got off the horse, Minnow looked carefully for the girl with red hair.

"Stay in the wagon," Pa told Rose.

Rose leaned out over the wagon seat to watch.
One horse had two riders, a man with a small
girl sitting behind him. Rose looked carefully.
It was the girl from the river.

Minnow slipped off the horse and walked toward the wagon. The red-haired girl cautiously climbed down. They both stood and looked at each other. Then, the red-haired girl grabbed a handful of berries from the bucket. She offered the juicy fruit to Minnow.

Minnow took the berries, popped them in her mouth, and smiled. "Minnow," she said, pointing to herself. Then she held up a long black braid. With her other hand, Minnow pointed at the girl's bright red hair.

The red-haired girl stepped back nervously. Minnow smiled and pointed to herself again. "Minnow," she repeated.

The red-haired girl smiled back. "Rose," she answered, placing her hand on her chest. "I'm Rose."

Minnow repeated the name, "Rose."

Suddenly, a man's loud voice called out harshly. Quick as lightning, Minnow raced back to her scolding father and scrambled up onto the horse.

Minnow's father had offered to help the pioneers cross the river in exchange for tools, and they had accepted. Early the next morning the two groups met at the crossing spot.

One by one, each wagon was unloaded and the wheels taken off. The empty wagon was lashed to a raft and reloaded. Using ropes, a team of oxen on the other side pulled the raft across the water. Then everything was removed from the wagon again. The empty wagon was taken off the raft and the wheels put back on. One last time, it was reloaded as the oxen were yoked.

As Rose waited for her family's turn, she kept
a lookout for Minnow.

"Come along, Rose," said Pa. "We're next."

"Did you see her, Pa?" Rose asked.

"No," Pa answered. "Maybe you'll see her tonight.
I have to take tools to their village to pay them for
helping us. You can come with me."

Rose climbed up on the wagon seat beside Pa. The
raft was slowly pulled into the water. It wobbled and
pitched, but Rose didn't notice. She was too busy
searching the far bank. The raft was about halfway
across when Rose spotted Minnow, hiding in
some berry bushes.

Instinctively, Rose stood up to wave. The raft
pitched to one side. Before Pa could grab
her, Rose fell into the rushing river.

Minnow had wanted to watch the wagons cross the river, but her father said, "No, you did not mind me yesterday."

Minnow watched the men ride away from her village, but then she followed them to the crossing spot. She hid in the berry bushes and looked for Rose.

At last Minnow spotted her, sitting on the seat of a wagon lashed to a raft. As the raft moved toward the middle of the river, she saw Rose stand up to wave.

Suddenly, the raft lurched. Minnow watched Rose fly from the wagon seat and disappear into the water.

It all happened so fast, Rose didn't even have time to take a breath!

Panicking, she kicked and flailed her arms but the strong rapids tossed her around and the weight of her dress pulled her down. Suddenly, something grabbed hold of her hair. Rose tried to get away, but she couldn't. The grasp was too tight and the water too powerful. Soon she was too exhausted to fight.

Minnow watched the long red hair disappear under the water. Quickly, she jumped in the river, dove under like an otter, and grabbed at the swirling hair. She caught a big bunch in her hand and hung on tight. Minnow tried to kick back up to the surface, but Rose fought her as much as the strong rapids did.

Just when Minnow thought she could hold her breath no longer, Rose's body went limp. Keeping a firm grip on Rose's hair, Minnow kicked with all her might and dragged Rose's head above the rippling currents.

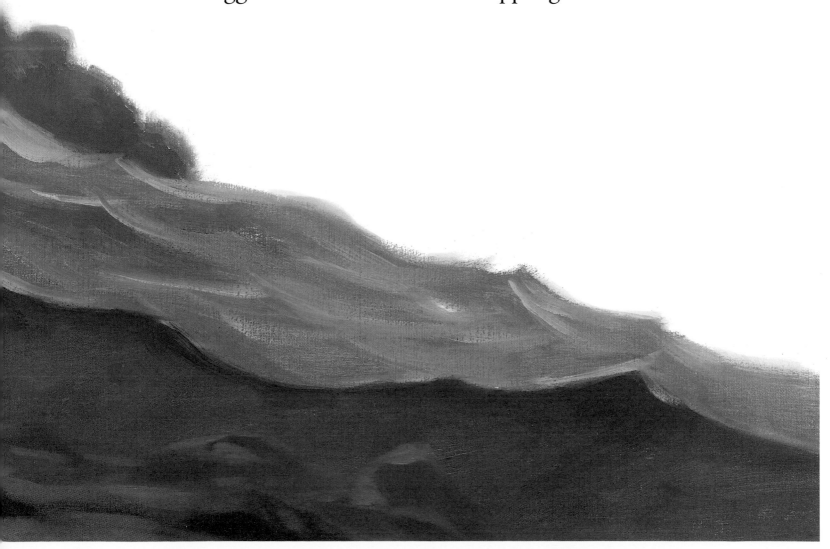

Rose coughed and gasped for breath but Minnow held
her tight. Together the two girls bobbed downstream
until the fast-moving waters poured into the calm pool.
Minnow kicked fiercely toward the bank until they
could touch bottom.

Then the two girls crawled out and lay totally exhausted
under the low branches of the berry bushes.

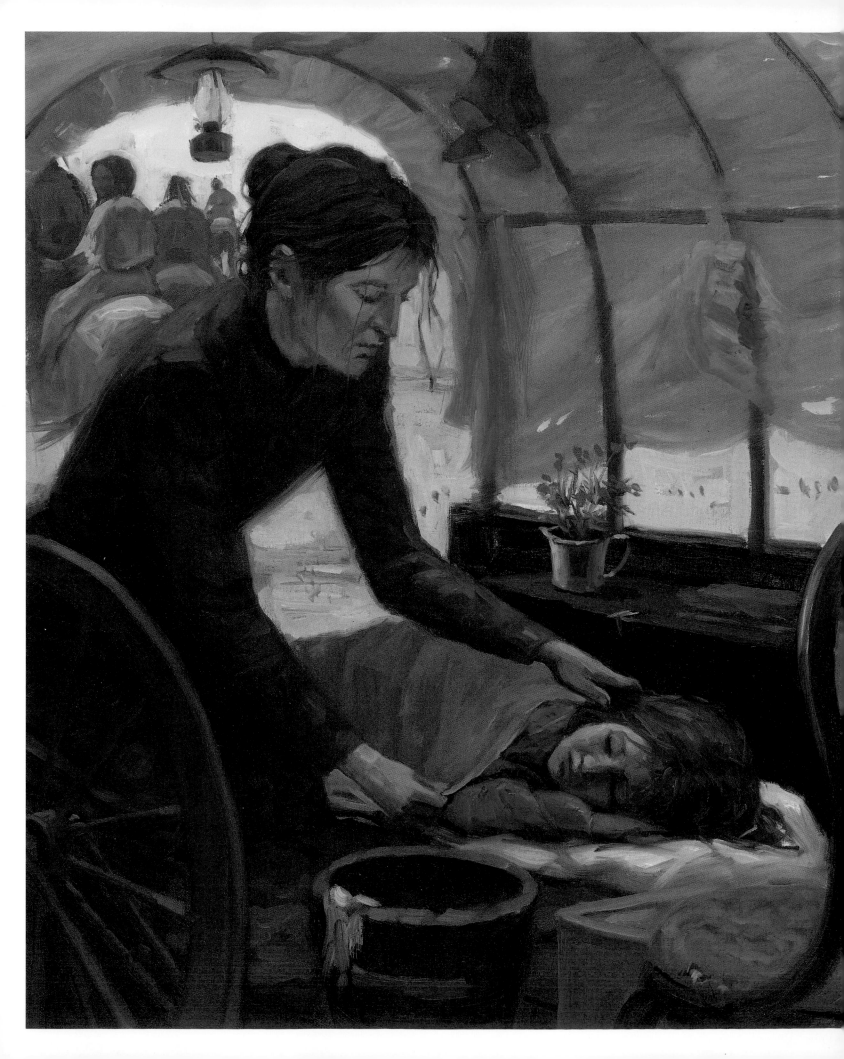

Everyone on the riverbank ran downstream, watching Minnow pull Rose to safety. They carried the two girls back to the crossing. Rose's distraught family, who had helplessly watched from the middle of the river, had just reached the far side.

Soon Rose lay snug and dry, sleeping in her wagon and Minnow rode back home, snuggled against the back of her father.

When Rose awoke later, her first thoughts were of Minnow. She wanted to give her something, not only for saving her life, but to offer in friendship. Mother baked a berry cobbler for her take to the village but Rose wanted something more. Something only she could give.

As she brushed her hair, Rose knew what it would be. She gathered bundles of dried grass. She folded and braided the grasses, then neatly stitched some colorful scraps of material around them.

"Perfect," she thought, "except for one last part."

Minnow was the hero of her village. She enjoyed the attention but her thoughts kept turning to Rose. They had only just met, yet after what happened at the river she felt a strong bond with the red-haired girl.

Minnow wanted to give Rose something of herself.
She slipped away to the quiet of the river to think about it.

That evening Minnow and Rose sat side by side. A big dish of cobbler sat in front of them. Smiles glowed on their faces and in their hands were gifts of friendship.